Gunny's
Short Stories
and
Life Lessons

Chris Island

Order this book online at www.trafford.com
or email orders@trafford.com

Most Trafford titles are also available at major online book retailers.

Printed in the United States of America.

ISBN: 978-1-4669-8386-1 (sc)
ISBN: 978-1-4669-8387-8 (hc)
ISBN: 978-1-4669-8388-5 (e)

Library of Congress Control Number: 2013903977

Trafford rev. 03/05/2013

 www.trafford.com

North America & international
toll-free: 1 888 232 4444 (USA & Canada)
phone: 250 383 6864 ♦ fax: 812 355 4082

PREFACE

THIS IS THE FIRST story I ever wrote. It was a requirement for a class I took while serving in the Marine Corps. The assignment was to create a biography of my service career for promotions, command staff level positions, and possibly, an obituary. As I wrote it, I realized how many things I had done in my life, how many funny anecdotes and life lessons had come from my experiences. So I share these stories here with you to take what you may and potentially give back to others.

THE CASE OF THE NAIL-CLIPPER THIEF

*S*HE WAS JUST A common housewife. The type that no one would take a second look at and everyone took advantage of. If they only knew. She had a mission every day, and if it was not done, then EVERYTHING failed. Commoners did not understand the labor it took to make the "day in and day out" happen. She was raised a certain way and that did not paint the picture of her life. She found a good man, but he had his faults. Things could have been worse. He had his own style, and they did not always agree. There was enough common ground for them to work on, and they managed to bang out a living that they could be proud of. He had a job that he could not leave, and so did she, but she had a fetish that needed to be sated. HER NAILS HAD TO BE PERFECT!

When he left on a mission, he made one fatal error—he took the only set of nail clippers. They said their good-byes at the airport, not knowing what was to come. When she got home and looked over the empty house, there was something missing. She walked through the house and tried to fill the gaps left by his departure. When she ripped the sheets off the bed from their last encounter, a trickle of blood dripped from a ripped nail as the sheets ripped away. The longing grew. A quick bandage would have to do for now.

When she woke in the morning with her lady parts still aflame, she quickly went about her duty and ensured that her nails were mended. Once she restored the broken nail, there was something else missing. She looked around and instantly knew what had happened. It was not there, and he had taken it! Was it too late? Could she find it? It had to be in the truck, and the truck was at the base! She had to get it back, but it would not be easy. Being of nimble mind, the plan began to unfold.

She was quick, she was agile, and they had no chance. The vehicle was parked in a compound with the security that rated the White House, but she had a mission. Silently she crept through the trees, waiting at every turn for signs that she was detected, knowing that at any moment she would be caught, the mission would be scrubbed. But she crawled inch by inch toward her goal, hoping and praying that he left it. Every few feet, she would pause to assess the security and make sure she left no sign that she was there, for if she was found out, the trophy was lost. There was a roving patrol that she did not know about, and the timing had to be exact for success.

In the next blink of an eye, her opportunity slapped her in the face. Ninja-like she jumped over the fence, found the truck, and picked the lock, and as she rummaged through the truck. A panic set in—that it was gone and there would be no hope of getting it back. The thoughts swirled, and the panic started to take root. How was she going to get it back? Her mind raced with options, but none made sense. She made her way home, and by the time she pulled her covers over her head, it was all but lost.

She woke to a very unwelcome doorbell at a much unexpected time. Without even having time for coffee or a scrunchy, she opened the door, and there he was! The son of a bitch, with the sun shining behind him, making him gorgeous, and the sunlight reflecting all her flaws. With his hand extended, he said in a tone that made her lower parts sweat, "Are these your clippers?" Her nails and her heart fell to the floor!

THE BEACH

AS MY EYES STARTED to open and the clouds began to scatter from my mind, I felt the abrasive rub of sand on my back and heard the crashing of the waves in front of me. The clearer my vision got, the more questions started to form in my mind. As I got somewhat aware, I found myself on the shore with just my board shorts on and a bikini top in my pocket. With the sounds of the waves reverberating in my head like a canon in a valley, the only thing I could do was jump in the water, one to deafen the sound and two to clean up my body from whatever debauchery I got into the night before.

When I came out of the water, what I needed was something to clear my head, and what better than the "hair of the dog." I found the nearest palm-covered bar and asked for the BEST morning-after medicine—a Bloody Mary or, giving the place I was in, a Bloody Maria. When the clock struck noon—of course, no one has a clock where I was—I looked up from the bar and perused the shoreline. That's when I saw her. The sun blinded me at first, and then the silhouette of her body was an eclipse of the sun. She glided up to me with the grace of an angel and took the stool next to me, and BY GOD, when my eyes could focus again, she was amazing.

Strawberry blonde hair and the bluest eyes you could ever imagine. She had on a bikini that would make Aphrodite herself green with envy. When she spoke, it sounded like honey. She had a girl-next-door look and a hint of fire in her eye as she told me her name was Sasha. She sidled up next to me, and you could smell the musk in the air. Whether it was her or me is still unknown. From then on, we let the devil take us, and the drinking and dancing continued until we found ourselves staring at the horizon, waiting for the green flash.

We talked and danced and sang the night away. As the bar was announcing "LAST CALL," we were SO not ready to quit. So we stumbled our way back down to the beach and found a comfortable spot. With the last songs from the bar playing in the background, we kept spinning and dancing to the rhythm. Then our eyes locked, and lust overcame.

Our lips met and our bodies entwined as we spun with the tempo of the music. As the music sped up and our tongues danced, the world slipped away. We fell into rapture and rolled in the sand. My mind flashed images of the beaches of Eden as the high tide started to wash over us. Quickly, we found ourselves dancing in the water and our clothes left on the sand.

As the flow of the waves brought us together, she wrapped her legs around my waist. We wrapped our arms around each other and kissed deep as we rode the waves. Our tongues began to dance once again, and with her legs around my waist, I naturally found her spot. As the lust washed over us like the waves, I slid inside her, and the rhapsody washed us away. We rode each wave again and again and again with every thrust of the ocean. I entered her. It had to be fated because it was like Neptune himself who was thrusting the waves in tune with our hips. The clouds formed overhead, and then our eyes met. Then as a bolt of lightning flashed across the sky, we climaxed with a final penetration as if we climaxed with the gods.

THE PROPOSAL

*I*T STARTED WITH A trip to South Padre. I just got out of a bad marriage and met a crazy motherfucker when I went to Texas. I was pretty sure I would have been in jail had I gone with him to spring-break in South Padre. That being said, it was the springboard for this story. His antics introduced me to a beautiful, intelligent, and crazy chick that took not only my heart but also my soul and my very being. When I got the courage to take the plunge into the holy institute of marriage for the second time, I was so nervous and pretty sure I was two beats away from a heart attack.

So I planned the time and place for when I would propose. It was a sentimental place from my youth that had borne the fruit of many fond memories. First was to introduce her to my family. Second was to shop and buy the ring amidst the happenings of a vacation for her and her sisters. Finally was to find a way to get a moment alone with her in the exact place that I envisioned.

Meet the family, check; get the ring, check; now how do I get her away to ask the question? After three days of sightseeing, she and her sisters needed a quiet night—score! Something needs to be bought from the store; I can go get it and take her with me, then take a detour and go to the perfect place for the important question. COFFEE!

I love coffee, and I so seldom get a chance for 7-eleven coffee. If I can get her to take a ride with me, it would all go perfect. SWEET! She agreed! Not knowing the area, I'm sure she was worried about where we were going, especially after we passed two 7-elevens on the way. But we arrived at THE SPOT, and we went for a walk.

It was cold and late, so there was no one around. In retrospect, she probably thought I had something else in mind. We chatted for a bit, and when I got the courage, I got down on one knee and popped the question. When she saw the ring and looked into my eyes, she said the thing that every man would want to hear: "The only way out of this is by death, suicide, or natural causes." I knew right then we would be together forever!

COMING HOME

AFTER THIS LAST DEPLOYMENT, he was just this side of exploding. The only thing he could think about was getting back to her. The touch of her skin and the smell of her hair were sending him over the edge. The boarding ticket said 1700, and that would get him home just before she went to bed. She had no intention of going to bed. Knowing he was on his way home was better than any infuse of coffee on earth.

Impatiently he waited for the boarding call, and she rushed around the house to ensure that everything was perfect. The flight was the last leg of a long journey home and was only for a few hours but seemed like an eternity. When the plane landed, he rushed to the baggage claim and did not stop to see if there was something missing. She was on the final tasks of cleaning the house and had a special outfit laid out on the bed.

When the taxi pulled up to the house, he felt the stirring and could barely pay the cabbie as he ripped his bag out of the trunk. When she saw the lights in front of the house, her legs went weak, and she suddenly got moist. Call it coincidence or kismet, but as the taxi drove off and he looked at the house, the air got so thick with musk and the clouds started to form so quick that it must have been an act of God.

As she walked up to the door, thunder boomed in the distance and lightning flashed across the sky. He opened the door, and she was standing there with a beer, a shot, and a smile. He slammed the door shut, slammed the beer, and with a deep breath, took in what she had on. The silk hugged her curves, and the color enhanced the lust in her eyes. He had no clue where she got it, but being away from home for so long, he didn't care.

The luggage was left on the porch; the dog ran for cover. Their lips embraced like it was the first time. Hands danced over each other as their eyes met. No words were said, and none were needed to be as their bodies embraced once more. The need to have their heartbeats next to your lover being so great that the rest of the world does not exist.

As the front door closed, another clap of thunder rung, and the flash of lightning shone so bright that it silhouetted their embrace for all the neighbors to see. He pulled her close in his embrace, ran one hand up and one hand down her back. Feeling his embrace almost made her lose control, and as his hands explored every inch of her flesh, her knees gave way and she fell into his arms.

As the storm grew, their clothes flew, and he picked her up as she wrapped her legs around him. It was all they could do to find the nearest surface, so he set her atop the kitchen table. Their passion swelled, and the sounds from the storm masked the sound of their bodies coming together. One final boom of thunder that shook the house sent them both over the edge. As the storm settled, so did they settle in each other's arms, both agreeing that this was one of the better homecomings.

A DAY IN THE LIFE

A DAY IN THE life of Gunny starts much like any other day for just about every other person, or maybe not. First, there is the annoying alarm clock. To this day, I still have no idea why I bought cheap; it's not like I can't afford something better. The sound resonates in my head and causes me to start each day in a bit of a fright, which kick-starts the annoyance gene in every cell of my body. This is usually followed by what I call the snooze-button reflex, but for my cheap ass, this only lasts for four minutes—FOUR MINUTES! Who the hell wants to snooze for four minutes?

This is promptly followed by the debate phase. A lot of factors are discussed during the debate phase. How bad do I really have to pee? How well did I sleep, and am I rested enough to work out? How cold/hot is it outside if I do get up to work out? How bad do I really have to pee? Can I sneak another FREAKIN' FOUR MINUTES in before I do get up? What would be the workout if I did work out? How bad do I really have to pee? After all factors have been weighed and measured, I get up to go pee and get ready to work out.

On the way over to the gym, the same rhetoric goes through my head as it does every day. *God, I hope the gym isn't packed. If that idiot is there, grunting his head off again . . . so help me! Wonder how bad my fat shakes when I am doing cardio?* After deciding what rigorous torture I will subject myself to for the day, I turn up my music and begin. My thoughts shift from doing the exercise the correct way and pictures of all the women that have come through my life. I often wonder how they felt about meeting me or if they ever thought about me at all. Then it sways to listing the ones that had good experiences with me and the ones that had bad. Then my thoughts go way off topic, and I get back on the bench and continue my workout, grunting my head off. The cardio portion of my workout gives me time to think about my life—where I'm going, where I've been, and why that douche bag blaring speed metal can't afford some earbuds.

After the workout, there is a ten—to fifteen-minute window where I have to try and find some breakfast. While deployed, the timing often does not allow me the luxury to get to the chow hall, and if I am lucky, someone has brought me a plate the night before that I can heat up. Once the foraging is completed, it's off to the shower and just about the only time my schedule is set to my advantage. Having the odd shift may not give me time to get my own chow. It does, however, allow me to shower when everyone else is on shift, and there is an endless supply of hot water. Picking out clothes while deployed is fairly easy as I choose from one of three pairs of cargo pants and a handful of polo shirts. Here, I take a minute or two while I ingest my daily regimen of vitamins and pain killers and assess the living tasks. When do I have to do laundry again? Where can I get my next meal? You know, the basic necessities.

The walk to work is short. The compound spans all about .5 mile, but the tired sinks in from the workout, and it feels like I just woke up. Of course, the first thing that needs to be done is make a cup of coffee. Life does not begin without coffee. Luckily for me, there is a certain body language about me that lets people know not to talk to me right away. I suspect a picture forms in their heads of the consequences of poking a sleeping bear. My counterpart for the day shift is kind enough to let the coffee set in before starting the turnover.

The shift goes well enough, not as many A-holes as there normally are, and I only yell profanities once at the computer.

About halfway through, things start to pick up and more people start to gather, as is the case whenever a big commotion starts. Not that there is anything for all these people to do, but everyone wants a piece of the action. A good nine hours later, things start to simmer down. The attitude has become solemn as the job continues on, and thoughts turn to the one individual that has taken "the final ride." The crowd that had gathered quickly disperses to begin preparation for upcoming events, and I return to my job and the task at hand.

After turnover, I take the small walk back to my room, set the alarm, and if there is time, watch a movie before nodding off to do it all again. A day in the life of Gunny, much like any other day for just about every other person, or maybe not.

PARIS

I WAS ON A trip to Paris with a few buddies of mine, and while we were sightseeing, I got bored off my ass. So naturally, I looked for the closest bar. I found myself in this café that was getting ready to open the bar up for the night traffic. I stuck around and watched the setting up, thinking anything was probably better than the historic venture my buddies had in mind. As things started to pick up for the night, she walked in.

A sleek, svelte goddess that seemed to float more than walk, she was gorgeous in a flowing gown that accentuated every curve of her body. I tried to hide my gaze but could not pull my head away from her direction. The bar had all but two seats available, so when she chose the stool next to me, I was taken aback. My mind was in a flutter as to what her intentions would be. Not speaking the lingo, I played it low.

As she pulled out a cigarette and asked me for a light, I informed her that I don't smoke, and then she confessed that it wasn't the cigarette she wanted. Flattered, we had a laugh and shared a glass of wine. She spun a tale that was so equal to mine that it was like she followed me throughout my life. The conversation flowed as smoothly and as abundantly as the wine; it was only natural that we head back to my hotel.

On the way there, the smell of lust coming off both of us was intoxicating, and it made us twice as drunk. We were a block away from the hotel, and she pulled me into an alley, slamming me against the wall and ramming her tongue down my throat with such abandon that I found the room in my trousers quickly vacating. As the dizziness of the wine flowed over me, mixed with the lust-filled adrenaline that flowed through me, I gave way to my primal nature.

Then she started to unzip me and went down on her knees. I felt her breath, and I knew I was on the precipice of heaven itself. As I fell off the edge, the animal in me took over, and I lifted her, pinned her to the wall, and there was no stopping me from making her mine. Our tongues began to dance like two snakes in the Garden of Eden as I started to gather her dance around her waist. My exploring hand quickly found how turned on she was, and it only spurred me on. I finished removing my trousers, then I spun her around and put my hands on her hips.

As I slid up her leg and entered her, we both succumbed to lust and continued to thrust upon each other again and again. Quickly the sounds of our lust reached the ears of passersby, and a crowd started to form. Between the wine, lust, or exhibition, I was not to blame for my quick finish. We straightened our clothes, she grabbed my hand, and we rushed off to my hotel room. When I woke and the fog cleared, I realized that what we shared was a serendipitous night, and then I wondered how I had ended up cuffed to the trestles of the Eiffel Tower with just my jacket gracefully covering my junk.

LEGUME BUNNIES

*H*ERE IS A LITTLE story of the time I was introduced to a magical species that, although has been around for ages, I just found out about a few short years ago. My wife and I were on holiday in Egypt and taking advantage of an afternoon in the sun with this British couple also enjoying a well-needed rest from the hustle of life. We were talking about where each other was from and what made us decide on this particular spot to rest up for the next leg in the rat race. When the conversation slowed, the gentleman asked us if we have ever seen the rabbits in the peanut. What an odd question, I thought and obviously became immediately intrigued. I looked at my wife to ensure that I had heard him right, and the puzzled look on my wife's face told me I had.

Of course, we inquired as to what a rabbit in a peanut was. You could see in the eyes of our lunch companions that it was a well-kept secret for most of their lives. The couple began to spin this elaborate tale of how legend tells the story of the magical creatures. So the gentleman leaned forward and reached into the dish of nuts sitting at the center of the table and began to rifle through it. He warned that shelled nuts are not the best hunting grounds for the tiny pixie rodents then picked out one of the whole peanuts. He cracked open the nut, and there at one of the ends of the legume, no bigger than the span of a pencil eraser, was this tiny body and two twitchy ears. My wife and I were beside ourselves. Never in our combined years have we witnessed such wonder.

Our companions were quite puzzled by our reactions. The knowledge of the elusive creature was as common to them as tying shoes was to my wife and me. We contended ourselves with the rest of our lunch and talked of what we all planned for the day, but I could not get the newfound discovery out of my head, and I had to learn more. The rest of our holiday went relaxing enough despite my insistent need to stop by every bookstore and library along the way to see whatever I could find about the rabbits. Most of what I found was information on how to grow, cultivate, and process *Arachis hypogea*.

In order to find the origin of the rabbits themselves, I had to delve into legend and lore, stories of mystical creatures in a time of faerie and magic. It turned out that these creatures are related to a similar species known as the springtime lagomorph. Much like *Homo sapiens* evolved from apes, the rabbit in the peanut evolved from wherever rabbits evolved. This particular evolutionary line developed in an underground environment. As in the termite and the mole, this species of rabbit developed survival characteristics for underground life.

These resourceful tykes draw their nourishment from the nutrients in the ground and make *Arachis hypogea* their homes. As the legume develops, the little rodent makes slight adjustments to make it more hospitable. They, like most animals, have a hibernation cycle that coincides with the harvest time for our delicious snack. In all my research and my entire Internet searching, there were no indications as to how the rabbits get into the shell of the peanut. Over the pounds and pounds of peanuts I have studied, there has never been any indication of how they penetrate the shell. One scientific explanation indicates that when the pedicel turns downward and buries itself in the ground is when the rabbit starts its selection for its underground habitat. One other means I dug up was in a book I found in this occult shop down a back alley in a small town in Northern Ireland. This dusty tomb hinted to the magical powers of the rabbits and a possible ability of teleportation.

The latter explanation, for me, would have more credibility. For how could you account for SOOO many people enjoying these delicious treats for so long? I would further submit that those with an allergy to peanuts also have some aver to the mystical. In any case, I encourage everyone, the next time you partake in the treat of *Arachis hypogea*, you stop and thank the little lagomorph that has kept it clean for your consumption.

A Full Eight Seconds

I HAD BEEN LOOKING for a vacation, and I knew the dogs could use the fresh air. It only seemed logical to head out to Blue Ridge for a camping trip. Showing up at the site, the monolithic trees and the flow of the creek had GOT to be the most majestic site I had seen in months. The sounds of the water flowing and the chirping of the birds quickly settled the tension knots in my neck. After camp was set, the dogs and I ate. It was about time I got some well-needed relaxation time.

I secured the dogs in the RV and headed out on a trail that I spotted as I drove in. The sun was just going down, so I wanted to explore a bit before I got some shut-eye. As tired as I was, it felt good getting some exercise, climbing the rocks and slopes of the Blue Ridge. Not more than ten minutes into my hike, I heard water flowing where it shouldn't be and had to investigate.

I climbed further up the trail and I saw this sensual woman showering with one of those camping shower bags, pretty sure she thought she was far enough in the woods not to be seen. When our eyes met, the thing that came to my mind to say was, *If I said you had a beautiful body, would you hold it against me?* Shockingly, a sparkle showed in her eye, and she gave me that come-hither look with the come-over finger and everything.

Her body glistened in the sun with the suds of her midshower, and her hair glowed strawberry in the sun as it beamed through the mountain canopy. Like a siren, she called me to her, and I could not get my clothes off fast enough.

When our flesh melted together, I looked into eyes so blue they would tempt the devil himself. The suds provided the needed lubricant, and as I became engorged, I easily slid up her thigh and penetrated. With a gasp, she wrapped her arms around my neck and her legs around my waist. I was overcome with the velvet lining of her flower that I had to lean on the tree where the shower bag hung.

As I regained my balance, I turned on the valve to the shower, releasing the water, and she started riding me as I stood under the water. The water flowed, she rode me, and I matched the rhythm of her ride. I began to build to release and realized I was the bull in nature's rodeo; I wondered who was going to break who, and as the water from the shower bag ran out to its last drop . . .

She thrust her head back, her eyes rolled back, and her legs clamped tighter around my waist. She raised her hand, threw her hair back, and screamed, "The full eight seconds."

With wobbly legs, I asked her name, and she said, "We'll do this again soon, and it's Jenn!"

So Angels . . .

I THOUGHT ABOUT THEM a bit recently and all the different interpretations—the sacred kind you read about in the Bible, the unseen kinds that get their wings every time a bell rings, the ones you hold dear for a lifetime, and the ones of such beauty they take your breath away, the famous idols and bands people look up to and perceive as angels but who hide behind a veil and are just everyday, normal human beings. So many different ideas of angels, and although all could be argued as valid, I had to think about what I perceived to be an angel.

The more I thought about it, none of the definitions seemed to exactly fit. So I started to take little bits of each and gave my definition a more down-to-earth flavor. In my view, why couldn't an angel be that scorpion that stings a patrol leader prior to going out on patrol, cancelling the whole operation and finding out the entire unit would have walked into an ambush? Maybe it is that panda in the zoo that makes someone pause to look for just an instant and delays that someone from stepping on a furry little creature running across the path. Maybe that interpretation is a tad broad, and that substantially multiplies the number of potential angels.

So let's dial it down a bit and try to list some of the angels in my life that have helped or bettered me in some way, at least the ones I can name. Of course, there are the lovely ladies of wrestling, brunettes and blondes alike, enduring ladder matches in the best outfits. A very ironically named angel I had growing up was my dog, Satan. That dog went through so much in my house, being fitted for whatever kind of hats that we had, clothespins clipped to his ears, and the socks on ends of his legs. Thinking back, that could possibly be why he always tried to get out and go on travels around the neighborhood. Whatever he endured, he was always there with a wag of his tail and a lick of the hand. There was the corporal I had, going through infantry training, who punched me in the back of the head during squad rushes and asked if I knew where my weapon was pointed. To this day, I never point my weapon at anything I do not intend to shoot. My third-grade teacher who was nice to me when it seemed no one was. She made me realize that there was something in me worth a damn even if I couldn't see it myself.

The major who, despite the lack of eloquence in expressing my thought, saw that I knew more about my job than most he had dealt with in the past. My buddy Chris was definitely an angel. He made sure I stayed out of jail on many rum-filled nights and traveled with little funds, putting more mileage on machines with wheels than could be counted in a lifetime. Who has not had that shrewish waitress at a restaurant that suggests you could stand to lie off the sauce—barbecue sauce, of course. My father for showing me what it takes to be a man even when it's not always the easiest thing to do. Then there was that time I was camping and got lost looking for the river, must have walked for hours in circles. When I was stark and the soles of my feet all swollen—I swear I had a triple blister on one of them—I stopped and made camp for the night. I woke to the sound of a woodpecker, and through the column of trees stood an elk that led me to the main road. Mostly because the river was on the other side of the road and the elk just wanted some water, but who am I to ask the motivations of an angel?

There were two angels that came into my life rather oddly on one of my deployments: One, although I have yet to thank, did a tremendous service and quite possibly saved my job. It was one of those times when a nice person tried to do the right thing for no reason, just that it was right. The second was an Irish lass from Missouri. She came into my life at a time when I had no one to talk to and was about to lose my mind with everything that was going on. She found me sitting alone and took the time to come over and say hello. Sometimes, that is all that is needed to get through.

I had a few angels of the heart. First was Stephanie Majoram, who gave me my first kiss in the backseat of an Adler and didn't tell anyone how bad I was. Then there was Timmi, who showed me how strong I could love and the evil that is bred when that love is scorned. Next was Jeannie, who opened my mind to the gentle touch of ecstasy and made me a better lover. Then I met Sally McGovern, the lead singer of a band out of France; she had a thing with dryers that defied some laws of physics. And who could forget Shan, a pole dancer from Waco, who taught me much about stability.

But the best angel to date is my incredible wife, whose patience and love is only exceeded by the good Lord himself. Not only has she put up with all my shenanigans, she has also helped me take all that I have learned in life and put the pieces into a better person overall. So no matter what your perception is of an ANGEL or whom you consider to be an angel, it is always good to stop and think about how many angels have come into your life. Maybe reach out and contact one and give a "thanks" for helping out. How many angels have you seen lately?

STRANGE PEOPLE

YOU MEET A LOT of strange people in life. Most of the time, you don't even realize how strange until years later when you think back and try to see how much your life really meant in the world. You can argue the nature-versus-nurture bit all day when talking about the lifestyle that people live, but I believe it's a person's natural curiosity that takes them places and makes them meet people that give them real life lessons.

My natural curiosity usually took me to those places less traveled, so to speak. Now you could say that it was the way I was raised with four sisters who loved to gallivant, trying to find themselves or just to get away from whatever. Or you could say that I was an explorer since the day I could walk which drove me. I say it was the insatiable need to find out how people managed within the less-than-fortunate realms.

That's where I met an exotic wild cat from the shores of Eden. One that made guys do a double take, stand up straighter, and fluff up their chests as she walked by and sent that tingling feeling to your happy place when she touched your arm. The first time I saw Dora, I was hustling a game of nine ball at this dive bar in Albania, doing pretty good too; and I was up 10,500 leke, whatever that amounted to in USD. But in retrospect, it was probably because everyone else noticed the cool breeze of fresh air that walked into the place, and I was still playing with my balls. Dora had a way of making any man think things of danger and would make him sweat in church just by glancing his way.

I was so engulfed in the game, I didn't even see her walk over toward me and put her drink on the table in the corner under just about the only lamp in the place. As she stood there, the light cast her in a glow like the spotlight on an actor in all their fame and glory. She wore a tight red dress and five-inch stilettos with metal heels that have pierced the hearts of more men than anyone cared to count. Why she chose to talk to a wannabe gambler like me I'll ever know. Maybe it's because I was the only one that didn't sprain their neck when she walked in or that even when she was within arm's length of me I still didn't notice. Maybe it was the way I was dressed in my board shorts, gambling Hawaiian shirt with racehorses and royal flushes print, and sandals. In any case, it was my lucky day when she asked me for a light.

As all the guys stared over at my direction, wondering what it was that she was attracted to, I got this sense of foreboding beginning to swell in the air. I mean, the way I was dressed, I looked like an alcoholic gambling reject from *National Lampoon's Midlife Crisis Vacation*. What could she honestly see in that? was the question hanging in the air. In hopes to lighten the mood (and not get my ass kicked), I lobbed a few corny one-liners at Dora in order to get a laugh. Either she could feel my impending ass-whooping or out of politeness, she laughed as she flicked the ash of her cigarette. As she did, her voice rang out through the bar like the horns of angels, which just put a smile on everyone's face. With a sigh of relief that all my blood would stay within my skin for the time being, we continued our conversation.

The talk started out small enough with the typical bar-room chatter you hear. "What do you do?" "Where are you from?" All of which became boring rather quickly; however, it did lead to more stories of past lives from both of us. It turned out that we both shared a natural curiosity, one that had led us to exciting occupations during our time on this blue marble. Dora told me about how she used to be an auctioneer, selling everything from caps to cars and from flags to furs. I regaled her with stories of when I was on ship and the countries I visited and the time I fell over the starboard side and the captain threatened to tape me to the bow if I wasn't more careful.

We talked about the different foods we had tasted throughout our travels. From ham pizzas in Hawaii to fresh pear soup in Maracaibo and dozens of other delicacies most have never heard of. As the talk of food continued, it naturally led to suggestive ways in which food had been enjoyed during our respective travels. To be quite honest, thinking of some of my adventures with food and seeing Dora in that dress had me yearning to liberate myself from the cage that was my board shorts. After some additional suggestions with various food options, we agreed to relocate to her place after a quick stop at a twenty-four-hour grocery store.

As she ushered me into her place, our bodies began to entangle, and we briefly came up for air to throw the first few articles of clothing on the couch. I took a cursory glance around to give me an idea of the inner workings of Dora and what may lie ahead for the night. There was a blown-up picture of a postage stamp hanging on the wall on one side of the fireplace and a framed poster of the musical *Fame* on the other. She had an old phonograph and a stack of records with Rachmaninoff playing softly in the background. We separated from each other's arms long enough to put the groceries in the kitchen and grab a few select items to start off the events of the night. She looked me in the eyes, and I could see the fire of lust, then she took my hand and led me to the bedroom.

The crescendo of the night came when I walked through the door of her bedroom. The right side of the room had a pulpit in the far corner with a crucifix standing seven feet tall behind it and a spotlight illuminating the face of Jesus and what could only be described as a couple of rows of pews painted on the wall. The left side of the room was painted blacker than the darkest night, with black lights strung across the entire half of the ceiling. Chains and leather straps were bolted to the walls, and various clamps, rifflers, and toys were hung. A huge timepiece brought the two worlds together. It hung over the headboard of the king-size bed dressed half in lace and frills, the other in black latex.

Curiosity or not, the cold shiver that ran up my back at that time was all the motivation I needed to end that little adventure. Grabbing my clothes and throwing them on, at a full sprint, I thought about how much money I had won at pool earlier and how lucky I was to dodge two occasions that could have had my blood leaked out. Well, as the saying goes, "Curiosity killed the cat." Thinking back now, I wonder if the other half of that saying would have proven true that "satisfaction brought it back."

NEVER EVER, EVER, EVER DRIVE ANGRY!

*I*T WAS A TIME in my life where things were going just so perfect that, you know, I had to do something to fuck it all up. I had a decent job, a nice Mustang GT, and a fine-ass girlfriend. Things couldn't get any better.

I was hanging out with two of my buddies one night while my girlfriend was working. Nothing special was going on, so something was bound to happen. We were just kicking it on the block, talking trash as most young men do, and I got the call.

The girl had called to say how hard her day went and that she was going home. Being the understanding guy that I am, I wished her a good night's sleep and said I would catch up with her tomorrow. Besides, I didn't want to fuck up my guy time.

As my friends and I were talking, the conversation came around to girls, as it usually does with guys, and one of them mentioned how my girl had been talking to her EX recently. "It's no big," I said, trying to be the bigger man about it. But the seed was planted, and it started to grow. About an hour later, I got a call from another friend who said my girl was out with her EX.

That was the push I needed. I spent the last hour with visions of her in her EX's arms for the past hour and getting madder by the minute. So the lot of us piled into my car and headed out. It was about forty-five minutes to an hour to drive to my girl's work, but I knew the 'Stang could get us there in twenty minutes.

So I got on the turnpike and head north, doing about 90 MPH. The pictures of her cheating on me in my head and me losing her just made the rage build up and the accelerator to go further to the floor. Zipping in and out of traffic like I was in the Sprint Cup at Talladega, I saw the nose of a cop car on the side of the road. By the time I got the sense to check my mirrors, all I saw was the light bar on the state trooper's car as it pulled on to the turnpike.

Now what the fuck was I going to do? I knew my license was already suspended for the two other times I got arrested for drag racing, and at the speed I was at, it was definitely jail time. Oh well, what's a man to do? So I floored it and hoped for the best. When I hit 110, I realized that there was not an exit for about twenty miles.

Then I thought, *There is no way I can outrun their radios.* They probably have three cars up ahead already waiting. I could see the fear in my buddies' eyes as I sped up to try and make it. The last thing I saw in my rearview mirror was the light bar disappearing as I raced around a bend. Then there it was, an exit I had forgotten about.

So I veered to the right to get off the turnpike. If I could get through the exit before the trooper came around the bend, I would be set. I came off the exit at about 85 and lost the steering wheel and headed into oncoming traffic. Pretty sure the guy behind the wheel of the headlights pointing at me shit his pants.

I quickly regained control and started weaving through the neighborhood. I could still hear the sirens as if they were behind me. I had to think quick. Although black Mustang GTs were common on Strong Island, New York, they would most likely stop any they see and question them. The way my heart was racing and the wide-eyed look on the faces of my buddies would definitely give me away.

Down the block, I saw a house whose owner had conveniently left the garage open and all the lights off, so I pulled into the garage and shut everything off just in time to see a state trooper fly by with his lights on.

We sat there, waiting for things to cool down and our pulses to get under control before heading back home and drinking a few beers. Afterward I realized how close I had come to dying and killing my buddies over a cheating slut. That was when I made a conscious decision to prioritize the things in my life; unfortunately, it took a couple more times of getting away from the cops to actually stick to that decision.

TWO SHIPS PASSING

S O AFTER MANY DEPLOYMENTS, he comes back to the States. Tired and with many memories swirling in this cowboy's head, he has a few hours on a layover that afforded him some time to himself. As he sits with his thoughts, trying to sort out what's what in life, the bartender asks what he wants. He orders a beer and a shot of whiskey so he can relax for the next leg of the long trip home. As he mulls over the past few months, she sidles up next to him. At first he doesn't notice, with the memories filling his mind, but then he catches her in the corner of his eye. A woman with such an innocent look that captivates the senses, ebony hair that betrays the true nature, and green eyes that takes his breath away. He is in awe and forgets his woes for a second, just long enough to ask her name.

When she answers "Jessica," she sees something in his eyes that peg him as a worried soul, and she wants to know more. So she asks where his destination is and where he came from. Sadly he tells her his story, that he came from overseas and was trying to get back home.

They share many stories and many drinks as their layover ticks on. As they look at their watches and realize that their time is coming to an end, they share a long look, and the mutual wonder overcomes them in the question, "If passion were fire, would the airport be ablaze!" That look gleams in their eyes, and they make a dash. Both looking frantically for ANY PLACE that will suffice, there they see it—a corner that no one is in and a place that is secluded. They share once more look into each other's eyes, and then their lips touch. He is blown away at how soft her lips are, and she is overcome with lust.

He falls back into a chair, and she falls on top of him, their lips never losing contact. Through his jeans, she can feel him getting engorged, and it spurs her passion. He is intoxicated with the mix of her perfume and musk. She reaches down and unzips his jeans and releases him. He lifts her skirt and accepts the invitation. As she slides him into her and as their tongues are entwined, they simultaneously let out a sigh of the purest ecstasy known to every humankind.

Passion quickly overcomes both of them, and in minutes, they are in the rapture of sexual bliss. Coming to, they realize that both their flights are about to leave and compose themselves with a straightening of clothing, peck on the lips, and a longing look to let each other know that neither will forget the glorious memory of two ships passing in the night.

The Tattoo Bet

So here I sit, another day at work. It has been a different experience, this being my first time as an instructor. Although my intel knowledge is vast, the requirements of the job are slightly different but nothing that I can't overcome. So while I'm here, I thought I would keep my imagery skills up by making bets with other analysts, mostly for coffee. Man, I love me some coffee!

So after a few bets and even more coffee, I had concluded that my skills are indeed legendary; and when I pass from this existence, my brain will be studied to unlock the secrets of greatness. As with any great individual in life, there are those that insist on trying to take them down. Thus is the case with this individual, a lovely woman in her own right but who did not comprehend the AWESOME POWERS of the GUNNY.

We had begun the contest with friendly banter within the chat rooms at work, where she had taken my jovial nature as a sign that the GUNNY POWERS were slipping. Unbeknownst to me was that this blossoming lily had possessed the amazing LADY GARGAR POWERS. A threat indeed, and when she challenged me, I could see a reason for concern.

However, a challenge is a challenge and must be answered, but with two almost equally powerful entities such as the Blossoming Lily and the Braying Jackass, a bet for mere coffee was not enough. No, the loser had to carry the evidence of defeat for all eternity, a mark to be reminded and never again question the other's ability.

So it was settled and a judge was selected, the judge being someone that had previously fallen at the mighty intellect of the GUNNY POWERS. The bet was a onetime event with the loser having to bear the symbol of the other for the rest of their lives. One assessment, one shot to defeat the other or reign supreme.

Then the game was underway. Each was given a time limit to make the necessary calculations and sift through the information to make their assessments. There I sat, pouring over all that I had been given and gathered unto me the furthest reaches of the GUNNY POWER to ensure victory. But in the back of my mind was the unknown, the "X factor," the question, what was the true power of the LADY GARGAR?

Can the GUNNY POWER truly overcome? These were doubts I could not afford to embellish on. I needed to focus and not let fear stop me from what needed to be done. So I analyzed and screened and sweated over all that was in front of me. *It had to be enough, it just had to be.* The thought rang out in my head over and over.

What is this? BL had made a quick assessment. Could her powers be that strong as to conclude the outcome this fast? Again, doubt crept into my mind. *NO!* I told myself I must trust in the GUNNY POWER. "Do not let fear of the unknown cloud that which you know to be true." Where the kung fu movie flashback came from I'll never know, but it was right. I just needed to have faith in the ALL-KNOWING GUNNY POWER.

So my assessment was made, and the two handed over to the judge. Now all that was left was the wait and with that wait the taunting and goading, trying to shake the other's faith in their respective awesomeness. Then a change, something was happening, something that could alter the outcome and something that could forever leave a question as to who truly is ALL POWERFUL.

The two titans discussed what should be done. Neither of which would give way and admit the other better, and so an agreement was struck and the game continued. The seconds went by to minutes, the minutes went by to hours, and then we heard it. Over the airwaves, it rang out for all to hear. The final decision was set in stone, written in the history books, and thus the loser so marked.

When the dust had settled and the air had cleared, I stood. Sweat-soaked body from the battle and barely able to stand, but stand I did as the victor to the TATTOO BET. As I think back on it, had I lost, I would have borne the mark of LADY GARGAR proudly as a symbol of the epic battle and of mutual respect.

THE WARRIOR WITH A CAUSE

ONCE UPON A TIME, there was a warrior. To some he was a hero, to others a raving maniac, and still to others a sage. Though there was nothing extraordinary about this warrior, there were those who would tell you he was meant for greatness. Others said he would end up in an asylum. Such is the balance of life. Throughout his life, there has been a struggle within him, a battle for which he could not pin down. As he grew, the urge to fight grew; and as he learned more in life, it took shape and began to have meaning.

He took up a cause against the sloths. Throughout his life, these creatures lurked everywhere and threatened the security and well-being of everyone that he held dear. These were not the ordinary, cute three-toed kind, but the menacing, ever-breeding monsters filled with complacency, stupidity, and triviality. Those that will always do just enough to get by, to just barely finish a job, whose motto is "That's good enough" or a variant of the same, and then believe they have actually done something good. These are the creatures that will be the downfall of civilization.

To be realistic, the world will always be plagued by these horrific creatures, ever drawing more and more to convert to their mediocrity. It is unfathomable to believe one lone soldier, one brave of heart can vanquish every last stitch of complacency. For even if others were to flock to the cause of progress and attempt to find new ways to do things better, it is just human nature to just get by.

But let's go back to the beginning where those life-committing decisions were made. As a boy, the warrior grew up with a little less than others around him. Always enough to survive and make it through the next day but having to make do and find new ways to utilize the things around him. Those with means would mock and ridicule him and others like him. He grew to loathe them and vowed to make more of his life. So the urge to fight was planted at an early age. Each day he endured new challenges, saddled with the jeers of those that had life easy, every challenge fueling the flame within his soul and forging the will to right the wrong of the small-minded.

As the warrior entered manhood, the flames within had become an inferno ready to consume anything in its path, but this fire threatened to consume the warrior and needed to be guided and focused. The military provided the direction and knowledge that honed the fire within. There, the warrior built his skills and learned to identify where the threat lived, how it survived, and the weaknesses of the sloths. As the warrior felt his skills sharpen and his focus intensify, he faced yet still more challenges from those that knew not the meaning of personal pride and the feel of a good day's hard work. On more than one occasion, the warrior had to dispatch the growing threat of a budding sloth trying to spread its vial ways.

For years the warrior battled hordes of sloths. Again and again he would throw himself into dens and slay as many as he could then retreat without being corrupted by their foul touch. Often the warrior would find himself so far deep into a den, there seemed to be no way out, and then he would have to rely on stealth and cunning to find a way back out of the hell he charged into.

Occasionally, the warrior would be successful in converting one of the sloths to the path of the righteous, and he hoped those he saved would continue the fight. Now as the warrior begins to weary and the fight seems to be a lost cause, he wonders if it is still worth the effort.

JUGGLING ACT

S O IT WAS A typical weekend night at the base, and at the time I was entertaining the company of quite a few lovely ladies. Not at the same time, mind you, although the thought did cross my mind. At this particular night, I was juggling three of them—one on base, one of the locals, and one from Dallas.

Usually, when I entertain, I dedicate all my time to my companion for that evening and no other. On this night, my "friend" from Dallas had come to San Angelo to visit, so I had to make unexpected plans. We met up with one of my buddies from the base and then went to the base club. The club was just like any other bar with pool tables, dartboards, and of course, a bar.

I had intel that my "friend" from base had gone out of town and there was no way for my local "friend" to get on base, so I figured it was safe to enjoy a night of drinking and dancing with my Dallas friend for the evening. So we got a pitcher of beer and started off with some darts. During the game, I found out that my Dallas friend is quite the pool player. Being from New York, I quickly came up with a plan to make some extra cash. It was a game called three ball. To all those that are in the dark, let me pull back the curtain.

For all those playing anti-$1, or whatever high roller you are, the one that sinks all three balls in the least amount of shots wins the pot. If there is a tie, then the pot rolls over and everyone puts in another $1. The plan was that I would go first and my friend would go last and match whoever was winning in order to roll the pot over.

So as the night went on, I talked quite a few people into the game, and the pot was getting pretty substantial. I, being the gentleman I am, put in the $1 for both my friend and me. After a few shots and many pitchers, we wrapped the game up and collected the somewhat large pot by this time.

When we got bored with this game, I set up for my shot. As I placed the cue ball on the table, I looked over at the bar and there, right in the middle of the bar, was my local friend and my Dallas friend. My Dallas friend noticed that I had seen her and took it upon herself to go say "HI." So here was what rang in my head, I was having a great night, looking to drink for free, made a few bucks, and made some cash with the pot I was fixin' to claim.

Needless to say, my concentration went to shit and I BLEW that last round completely. At that time, my mind was scrambling—or is *rambling* a better word?—with no explanation. I lost the round and All THE MONEY I had in the pot, and with the huge bar tab, it was a pretty rough lesson to learn on juggling friends.

Just goes to show that you can fall "on top of the world," but there will always be something that sets it afire and burn it down.

THAT TIME IN MEXICO

*H*OW MANY PEOPLE ACTUALLY look over their bad experiences and try to find the lessons learned? Can't say it would be many—you can probably count them without taking your shoes off—but isn't that why they say "History has a way of repeating itself"? I mean to truly break the cycle of making the same mistakes over and over. Every aspect of our lives should be scrutinized to successfully move forward. Hell, I sure don't like looking over my bad decisions. Lord knows, there are quite a few to look at too. But sometimes that is what's needed to see how not to wind up between a rock and hard place.

I had this TERRIBLE week at work while I was stationed in Yuma, Arizona, the kind that makes you want to kick puppies and throw furniture. So I decided to go shoot off some steam with some buddies out in town. We figured we'd hit a few bars and after I'd have time to cool down from the week's torture fest. The night started out well enough; I had a few beers, shot some pool and darts, even managed to chat up a couple of hotties without venting the frustration I had left over.

We hit a couple of clubs, and I managed to keep a smile on my face; but I was a man on a mission, as they say, and was tending to drink a bit. As the night was coming to an end, my friends were getting the sense of calling it and go home, but I persuaded them to make one more stop at a small bar I had noticed earlier in the week. It looked like a hole-in-the-wall, but it was out of the way and looked quiet enough for a couple more games of pool and another shot or two to wash any residual anger I had from work. Given our current state, we thought it best to hail a couple of cabbies and wagon over to the last stop for the night. That was probably the last good decision I made.

Getting out of the cabs, my buddies got that cautionary feeling, setting off alarms that made you fear for your safety. You know, the kind you get when you see someone standing too close to the tracks when a train is coming? I took their hesitation as weakness, pushed my way to the door, and corralled my friends in while questioning the measure of their manhood. The bar was not too crowded, maybe three to five guys and three beautiful Mexican women spread throughout the bar. The bar had a distinct mantra to it, but we outnumbered them. So let the games begin.

I was feeling generous, so I bought the house a round. As I motioned for the bartender, my thought was to make sure my bad week was behind me. The bartender brought out a strange, dusty old bottle from under the counter and said, "A special occasion deserves a special drink." As the house rose our glasses, I gave a toast, warding off future misfortune and as I slapped the shot back, I caught the smile and the trademark look in the eye of the bartender that said he knew what was about to happen.

The guys and I drifted to our separate corners of the bar, a couple taking a last chance at the ladies for some companionship. Some were playing pool, one playing darts, and I just sidled up to the bar next to this one guy that looked like he had a worse week than I did. After some pleasant conversation, I realized that he probably didn't speak English. It was evident because he just nodded at everything I said. My friend and I had a couple more of the bartender's special shots; each raised the exponent of my buzz by three. My comrades would come up to me every now and then to see how I was doing, and each time they approached, they would multiply in my vision. I didn't see much concern in so long as I directed my conversation to the middle copy, which was the clearest.

The room started to spin, so I figured a trip to the bathroom was in order before there was an eruption of one kind or another. So I caromed off a couple of buddies and a couple of chairs and found the welcome door with a starfish on it and the word *HOMBRE* under it. I noticed the pelmet over the front window that still flashed the neon beer sign, even though it was well past closing, as I opened the door. Stepping through, I had to blink as the room opened up to this TV studio set. I looked back at the bar and back to the studio then back to the bar, and saw another special shot sitting at the end. With my head spinning, I figured, why not ride this out? So I slammed the shot down and stepped into the studio.

The set was made up to be some marketplace in Macedonia, and Lindsay Lohan was standing in the middle, reading a manuscript titled "Strutting the Way to Europe." She was standing, with whom I assumed was a casting assistant, in front of the band, talking about the next scene with a guy holding a Fender. There was a snack table for the crew with various muffins and tuna salads with notched-leaf lettuce. In the makeshift night sky of the set, I could make out Antila, Hydra, and Pyxis, all of which were completely inaccurate for Macedonia. The marketplace looked authentic enough with a plant here and there and numerous extras commencing in trade. Looking around, I kept seeing my buddies in random places and tried to figure what kind of time warp or dream I was strutting through in my attempts to find the bathroom.

I looked up in the rafters and saw that a vireo got stuck inside the studio, just as I was almost run down by a stagehand racing by in a Rudra T-shirt, roaring his head off and pushing a clothes rack full of costume rags and jackets. I started to heat up and was going to track the dude down when one of my buddies snapped me out of the odd vision by grabbing me and throwing me into a truck. We drove for so long that I finally succumbed and passed out. When I woke, I was sitting in a lawn chair on the corner of a Tijuana marketplace with a shopping cart full of oranges and the letters G-O-R-E written on my forearm.

As my eyes focused, I realized that all my money, my wallet, and my ID were gone. My clothes were torn, and my boots were replaced with flip-flops. The concrete was so hot, the heat made my knees sweat, and I was full of relief when I looked past the tennis shop down the road and saw a sign for the GORE Hotel. A quick walk down the road gave me time to contemplate the events that just passed and what I could learn from it. Don't drink angry. No. Know when to say enough. No, got it! Never drink special shots from a smiling bartender with a bar full of Mexicans and friends out to play a joke.

DALLAINIUS

*O*NCE UPON A TIME, there were four sisters, and these sisters ruled over the enchanted land of Dallainius. Dallainius is not located on any map. The only way to find Dallainius is to follow the setting sun to the far west until you reach the shore. There on the beach, you will find a bridge that spans out past the horizon. At the entrance to the bridge sits a peach-colored double-wide trailer with astro turf for a lawn and a pink flamingo stuck in the ground by a mailbox post in need of serious repair. Within this abode lived a huge sumo wrestler named Agnes. Agnes, as it turns out, was Dallainius's only security system, for it was well-known through all the lands that Dallainians were good-natured and desired to make new friends.

Under the rule of the four sisters—Rudonia (the temptress), Wendrina (the trusting), Sonyowsa (the wild), and Adelicious (the motherly)—the land thrived, and everyone within the land never wanted for anything. The four sisters were very fair indeed, each one more beautiful than the next. Their beauty was so well-known that suitors from all over swarmed to bask in their splendor. Their attributes did not stop with their looks for with the rigors of running the kingdom was met by their resounding commitment to excellence. The sisters spent many an hour struggling to keep the land of Dallainius a strong and prosperous place for all. Their only desire was that everyone lived long and happy lives with perfect teeth. Weekly the sisters would celebrate life with all the people of the land and often travel to far-off lands in search of new ways to bring joy to the inhabitants of their beloved land.

These travels were not without dangers, but instead of taking the security of Agnes away from Dallainius, they believed that the good nature of those they encountered would keep them safe. This attitude proved to be true for all but one travel to the nearby island of Sopadros. Sopadros was known to host a festival every year just after the winter season. This festival was almost as well-known as the sisters of Dallainius. The sisters gathered around every band and every group to sample as many of the joyous customs, the local food, and beverages in hopes of finding new items to bring home and spread around to their people. One parlor, decked out in a tropical setting, had beach toys tacked to the walls with neon-colored shovels and pails glowing in the black lights that illuminated the room. There was a resort bar that had a long hall at the entrance, and as you walked through the door, there was sand you could run your toes through. Then the walls were painted the color of the ocean, and as you walked down the hall, you would feel as though you walked closer toward Davy Jones's locker. As you entered the bar, there were various paintings of things you might find at the bottom of the ocean. An anchor with the Navy seal sat in the sand with a broken chain, a few signs of the zodiac Cancer flitted across the bottom of a water tank, and the bar itself was covered in part of a seaweed-tangled net with a mermaid cradled as if in a hammock. In order not to forget any of these ideas, once the trip was at an end, the sisters expended copious rolls of film.

All seemed to go well enough until the sisters' beauty caught the eye of a wolf in sheep's clothing. Marion, as the wolf was called, came from Mauna Kea and enjoyed visiting any place that boasts a good time. For it was in his foul nature never to secede from anything that had a guaranty of raucous laughter and the possibility to have his will be done, to which his range of depravity knew no bounds. One could say that the of the sisters' good nature was only a matter of time for this negative pariah.

When Marion found the attractive sisters, he immediately set upon exploiting them for any dastardly pleasure he could imagine. The sisters, with their intelligence only matched by their beauty, were not readily fooled by Marion's approach, and it seemed nothing would hamper his resolve. Again and again, Marion would seize the window of opportunity at every turn and was sure he would wear the sisters down. Marion's persistence tore at the seam of the bond between the sisters. When one of the sisters fell prey to the wolf's cunning, it was natural to assume Wendrina would let her trusting nature win over her better judgment, and they spent the next few weeks gallivanting hither and to. The other sisters did what they could to dissuade their misguided sibling and oft gave a piece of their minds to no avail.

Marion had a friend, a gentle giant of sorts that recently had a rough breakup with a vicious harpy from the northern lands. Grunus was still reeling from the separation and did not have a very positive outlook on life for putting him through such torture. When Grunus met Marion, he was seduced by the feeling created by Marion's evil ways, and the two became good friends rather quickly. Grunus and Marion traveled across the lands, looking for mischief and the pleasures of many women. The two would spend days at a time corrupting the minds of those around them and bend them to their will, leaving a swath of casualties inflicted with hangovers, memory loss, and for the select females in the path of the whirlwind, a satisfied feeling and sore legs. Through all the good times and adventures, the two would rawt across the land, but nothing seemed to either fill the hole in Grunus's heart or heal the emotional scars left by the harpy.

Then one day, as Grunus and Marion were resting and trying to decide the next adventure, an idea presented itself—an advertisement for a festival in Dallainius. For Marion, the choice was simple. The lure of another event to spread his mischief and to taste the sweet nectar of the lovely Wendrina all at once was too much to resist. Grunus needed some, but not much, persuasion to make the trip. Once Grunus heard the stories of the splendor of Dallainius and heard of the unsurpassed beauty of the sisters, he was all but fastening the seat belt in the chariot, ready to go. Grunus and Marion gathered as many brave warriors to attend the festival and boasted it to be the event of the century. As everyone arrived at the festival and Grunus set his eyes on the sisters for the first time, he felt a fresh, different feeling stir within, a feeling he had not felt in a long time. It was a feeling he felt he should know but could not put a finger on. It seemed to stir in the core of his body. Not being familiar with the feeling, Grunus shook it off and commenced to let the good times roll.

Throughout the festival, Marion spent most of the time with Wendrina, and Grunus took the rest of the warriors in search of their own brand of mischief. A glorious time was had by all during the festival, and to no one's surprise, Grunus and Marion were looking to move the party to wherever it could go. The exquisite hostesses that they were, the sisters recommended a remote section of Dallainius where the various customs and drink concoctions that the sisters brought back from their travels were tested. So the caravan of partygoers traversed to Debellium, and the whirlwind of chaos continued. Grunus and Marion were content with imbibing at one of the establishments and challenging each other to some tavern games of skill. The other warriors, having heard their own strange and wondrous tales of Dallainius, wanted to seek proof for what seemed too strange to be true. Rudonia, who seemed to be the one most sober, took the lead to show the truth in the rumors about her beloved land. As Rudonia gathered those who wished to experience other sites, she came upon Grunus, and for what seemed to be an eternity, everything stopped. The feel in the air seemed to change, the attitude of the people within a five-meter radius changed, and you could sense the inevitable collision about to happen.

There have been stories about when two forces collide, and this would make them all pale in comparison. Worse than two rams fighting for a mountain with each crushing blow echoing across the mountain range, more brutal than Zeus's battle with the titans, and twice as enthralling as watching someone standing too close to the train tracks, people watched as the initial encounter between the temptress and the giant stood frozen in time. As they parted—the result of the bout to this day still in question—and time returned to normal, the masses went about their frolicking and merriment. True to form, Grunus and Marion had left bodies strewn about, heads pounding, and memories running for the hills, never to be recovered.

Somehow Marion managed to convince Wendrina to host breakfast, partially for the fact that Marion promised to cook. Outside of his scoundrel ways, he actually cooked fairly well. No doubt a skill used in order to manipulate unsuspecting prey. As they sat down to a meal of eggs and pancakes with powdered sugar, they went about recalling whatever memories were too slow to make it out of their mental reach. As the stories progressed, reference to the encounter of Rudonia and Grunus began to dominate the conversation. Marion was quick to the side of Grunus, expounding on the numerous adventures they had shared and the triumphs of his friend. In turn, Wendrina and Sonyowsa regaled the group with Rudonia's victories; and as one thing led to another, the challenge was set. Eyes locked, Grunus and Rudonia established the proverbial ring in which to battle.

The competition went on for months, neither willing to let the other gain the upper hand. Each time they met for battle, that strange feeling continued to grow within Grunus. Eventually, he realized want it was. Giants were never known to be quick of wit, and it didn't take long after that that you could not separate the two. Grunus spent months of new moons chasing after Rudonia, and like the Welsh king Pweyll chasing Rhiannon, she was always one step out of his reach. Rudonia had fallen just the same for the gentle giant and enjoyed seeing how far he would go to show his love. They stand together to this day and have had many adventures of their own, but that is another story.

THE PNL BRIEF

OKAY, SO AFTER I went through imagery school, they thought it would be a good idea for some cross-service training to have a few of the marines go through the air force basic intel analyst course. I was one of the lucky ones. So we had about a week to fuck off while waiting for the next class to kick off. I, like the other lucky ones picked for this endeavor, spent that time clubbin' and keeping score on the locals and lovely air force women that we had the pleasure of sharing the company of.

When the class kicked off, none of the marines were in the frame of mind to do any kind of studying or to learn anything of value. But we all grabbed our morning joe and made our way to the first day of class. The course began pretty much the same as many other classes, with orientation and pleasantries. "Hello, this is me, this is where I'm from, and this is why I'm here." "BLAH BLAH BLAH, what time does the club open?" was the only thing going on in my head. So the days moved along with parties all night and drinking enough coffee during the day to stay awake and wash away the hangover. Then there was the long-awaited nap during chow, you know, to charge the batteries for that night's adventure and however many women wanted to party.

Then there was the class on briefing. The class was given because you have to ensure that as an intel analyst, you can give an intel brief to a commander effectively. This was where marines needed to come with a "parental warning" label because we brief marine commanders way different than the air force briefs their commanders.

So the first brief was on a topic of our choosing, and to the credit of the instructors, they ensured that the topics where informative and appropriate for all attendance. You can hear the whisper from all the marines in the back, "Well, fuck! Now what the hell am I going to talk about?" The day of briefings was upon us, and with me being the assistant class leader and a marine, the class thought it appropriate to start off on a good foot and had me give the first brief. Little did they know that I had just gotten back to base like three hours before from the some chick's house—what was her name?

Anyway, I was like five minutes late for class, still half-drunk, and when I got in the classroom, I had three air force NCOs up in my face, asking me "What happened?" "Why are you late?" "You have to give the first brief." "The instructors will be here soon." As God is my witness, it took everything I had not to punch every one of them in the face and go back to bed. So I gathered myself as calmly as possible and told them to just let me get a cup of coffee and everything will be okay. I proceeded to get my coffee and gather my notes for the brief, and just as I was about to go to the podium for a dry run, the instructors walked in and said, "Okay, who's first?"

So since I was already at the podium and that was the plan anyway, I took a sip of coffee, and with a motivated voice, I said, "Let's do this!" My brief was on the point of no learning (PNL), which, believe it or not, has a medical term. Don't ask me what it is—I have no clue. So there I was, going through my notes like a freaking pro! Like I have been briefing since birth, there were medical references, and I even had a visual aid, which was one of those NERF brain footballs, which I illustrated that as the brain fills up with knowledge during class, there comes a time when nothing else will fit inside the brain.

I totally rocked it! At least that was what was happening in my head, since I was probably still drunk and could have blown a 0.24 had they given me a breathalyzer. The entire class got stoned off the alcohol coming off me, and I was close to passing out by the time I was done.

I looked up after I finished, and the instructors had this look of amazement on their faces, eyes wide open and jaws hanging down. I took this as approval only to find out that they passed me for just having the balls to get up in front of the class and go through with it in the condition I was in. Even the other marines in the class were like, "How the fuck did you pull that off?" Sometimes you just have to do it.

My Guiding Light
is a Felon

*L*IKE MANY OTHER MEN and women across this great nation, I heard the call and answered. For me, enlisting in the service was more of a necessity than a calling. I was going on twenty-one and had no intention of furthering my education. That is how they track you! But I was tired of living under my parents' roof and needed a way out.

So I decided one day to listen to the federal propaganda and see what options it offered. I spent some time with all the recruiters and was not impressed. The last one I saw was the one least available, and it vexed me. When I met him, there was an air of arrogance and a confidence in him that set me on edge. But I was determined, so I asked the question, "What's this all about?" He looked me up and looked me down and took a deep breath and said the last thing I ever expected: "What can you do for the Corps?" From that day on, I was signed up.

Going through twenty years and looking at it now, I can say it looked nothing like it did back then. But like the mullet I wore in the 1970s, some things have to change. So to boot camp I went and a stereotype I upheld. Most of those that served during my time ended up marrying a dancer with two to five kids and fell in love with the first set of breasts they saw. I took the other route, which was to realize that the girl you spent your last night of freedom with, you left something behind.

We made a go of it, but we both knew our hearts were someplace else. We created four blessings, and I regret every day that I was not there for them. But life moves on, and so move on I did. I saw a bumper sticker once that said, "I was not born in Texas but I got here as soon as I could." That was where I found the light of my life. We hit it off like every great relationship, and we couldn't stand the sight of each other. It was a night of partying and experiencing new things; no judging and much fun was had by all.

She is amazing in so many ways, beautiful, intelligent, and with a spirit that could light the world, or at least a big city. We have both traveled literally around the globe twice, once by ourselves and then together. She has taught me so much and has made me into a better person than I ever could have reached alone. My only hope was to keep her safe and that any part of me has enriched her life as she has mine. But through our lives, and like most people, hard times hit and things got heated. The one thing that kept us moving forward was our devotion to each other.

Fast forward through a WHOLE LOT of drama, and we actually started to make things work. We come to the latest dilemma that happened on my return from overseas on the last deployment of my active career. I came home a day early, and she was preparing for a HUGE welcome home. I wanted to surprise her, so I did not tell her I was coming. She was getting the house ready, and the anxiety was overflowing; in order to take the edge off, she imbibed a bit. So when I called to say, "Hey, I need a ride home," she was a bit over the legal limit.

She didn't seem that bad, but the funny thing was, when she got on base, she didn't know where she was going and stopped for directions. Now that may not seem funny, but the place she stopped to ask at was the only military police station on base. Now you would think that all the cop cars in the parking lot would have been an indicator, but that could be explained by a possible shift change, and they were just comparing notes.

But when you walked into the building and saw all the guys in police uniform, something should have set off alarms. It seemed she was so hell-bent on getting me back that everything else didn't matter.

Now getting pinched for being over the limit is not a death sentence, but being that it happened on a military base makes it a federal crime and bumps everything up to a felony. When we had the hearing on base, the one presiding even said there was a time that a spouse caught driving under the influence on base would be left to take care of at home. But things change, sometimes for the better, sometimes not, so she can no longer drive on base and has a felony record for picking up her husband after a deployment overseas. Such is life. For those that will read this, be aware, ANY offense committed on a base is considered a felony crime in civilian life.

ALWAYS LEARNING

*D*URING MY TRAVELS, I had the rare opportunity to witness a very interesting thing. I met this one creature on one of my travels, and it was one of the more memorable times. During my life—and for some reason, it happened at a time that I wanted the least to do with anyone—I was reminded of how we, humans, can still learn no matter what is happening in our lives or how old we are.

This creature was small in stature but extremely agile as he jumped around on every surface within a ten-foot radius. As I watched it, I was amazed at the agility and the energy in which he bounced from one surface to the next with such ease. He redefined everything I knew to be true about the laws of gravity. I was so upset with my life that it took me a couple moments to realize how amazing this creature was.

I would sit, watch, and wonder if there was something I should do. But something in the back of my mind said I would interrupt this creature's way of life if I did. I attempted to reach my hand out in supplication, and with that simple gesture, a friendship was born. Over the next couple of days, I would see it watching me and at times mimic my actions. As I sat one day, studying this creature, I wondered who the parents were.

Turned out I had the very fortunate account of meeting the creators of this creature earlier in my travels, one rather large male that was prone to biting and a female that had a glint of intelligence in her eye that I found extremely rare. We had interacted on many occasions, but this time was the first time I had met their offspring. Knowing who the parents were, I knew instantly that the agility and the energy within this creature was magical. It had to be the only explanation of the gravity-defying feats that this creature preformed.

Our first meeting was brief, but I had close ties to its parents and knew we would meet again. I spent the next few days thinking of a logical reason of how this creature could jump and fly through the air. It had the characteristics of a flying squirrel and spider monkey all wrapped up in a blonde-haired blue-eyed I-don't-know-what, and my curiosity tremendously peaked. Since then, I have been traveling SOOO much, it has been hard to tell what time of day it is, let alone who I meet. But this one encounter stuck in my head, and it reminded me of how small encounters can influence, like ripples in a pond from a pebble.

The second time I met this creature, I had the blessing of meeting another wonderful creation. It was SOOO much smaller and bounced around like a ball in a pinball machine. It took everything that the parents had to make it settle for two seconds and acknowledge that someone else was in the room. She was way smaller obviously and had these curious eyes so full of wonder and yet made you think about what was going on in the mind behind those eyes. Was she learning about life, or was she looking for a way to get what she wanted? Growing up with four sisters, the first thing I realized was that, with females, it is usually one and the same.

This new creature acted so sweet and playful but, when I stopped playing, threw a fit that would rival King Kong himself. Visiting with the family, I witnessed a life-affirming constant most people often forget—no matter the age, we can all learn from each other. I watched the father teaching the son how to bring supplies to the home on my last visit. The path that the father took was a direct route, and he lugged the heavy objects up over a very arduous embankment. The son just stood there and watched, and it seemed that he did not understand the concept. As the father started to become enraged at the son's inaction, the son picked up one of the heavy objects, walked a slight distance around the embankment, and delivered the supplies to the home with half the effort. In the numerous times I watched the parents teaching the smaller creatures about life, it was a gift to see the wonder in the eyes of the father when the son showed him a better way of doing things.

FEARS

S O I HAVE BEEN spending the last few days looking over my shoulder. I have no reason to, and there is certainly no one chasing me; I don't think there is anyway. So why do I have these feelings of dread and keep seeing people out of the corners of my eyes? I remember when I was younger and I had these feelings. I would get scared over stupid things, and one day I said, "Enough is enough."

So I started to define my fears and research them in order to try to understand each one of them. The first is aquaphobia, which to this day still vexes me. I remember having dreams of me falling out of a boat and being weighed down by what I could not say. I would just keep sinking deeper and deeper. So I forced myself to learn how to surf and later in life learned how to scuba dive. Since then, I have had a great time diving. I swam with a sea turtle on my birthday while in Okinawa and later that day got chased by a sea snake, and I have swum with tiger fish in the Red Sea off the coast of Egypt. The fear rears its head every now and then, but I think about those times and it is not as bad.

When I was little, I had achluophobia and had to sleep with some kind light, any kind of light. The door open, a night light, or sometimes both was needed for me to go to sleep. Also, while playing hide-and-seek, I found that I couldn't pick some of the really good places because I suffered from claustrophobia. I used an old saying for these and killed two birds with one stone. So I would lock myself in a room, turn the lights off, and just sit in the middle of the floor. When the anxiety started to brew, I started to just breathe, nice and slow, deep and steady. I would spend hours at a time until the fear subsided.

At times, I would feel severely uncomfortable when I was in crowded places, which I later identified as agoraphobia. As I neared my high school graduation and wanted a car but had no money, I took the worst job anyone suffering from agoraphobia could take. I went to work in a carnival—yes, I know. As well as the amount of people freaking me out, there were all the regular freaks associated with a carnival. So when it started to affect the job, I started to go to clubs—the more packed, the better. Overcoming that fear didn't do much for my social skills, as it turned my fear of people into anger, and now I consider everyone an annoyance.

The last big one was necrophobia, which I think all people have to some degree. But when I felt this fear started to take root, I decided to nip it in the bud. I joined the military and went through the training and conducted missions that made me face that fear. Again, it is still there to some extent, but after all the training and experience, it is not such a big deal.

There will always be something to be afraid of, but there is no reason to let it take over my life. So now there is this new feeling; I suspect that it has something to do with the lifestyle change of being out of the marine corps. Seems to be time for some self-reflection and possibly new fears to face. It is simple—just face your fears.